ON MOTHER'S LAP

ISBN 0-590-46889-8

Text copyright © 1972 by Ann Herbert Scott.
Illustrations copyright © 1992 by Glo Coalson.
All rights reserved. Published by Scholastic Inc.,
730 Broadway, New York, NY 10003, by arrangement with
Clarion Books, an imprint of Houghton Mifflin Company.

12 11 10 9 8 7 6 5 4 3 2 1   3 4 5 6 7 8/9

Printed in the U.S.A.   09

First Scholastic printing, November 1993

For Kate
A.H.S.

**For Jewel Ross Bowles and
LaVerne Bowles Coalson**
G.C.

ON MOTHER'S LAP

By Ann Herbert Scott

Illustrated by Glo Coalson

SCHOLASTIC INC.

New York   Toronto   London   Auckland   Sydney

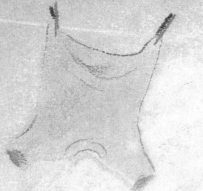

Michael was sitting on his mother's lap.
Back and forth,
back and forth, they rocked.

"Let's get Dolly," said Michael.

Soon Michael and Dolly were on Mother's lap. Back and forth, back and forth, they rocked.

"Boat needs me," said Michael.
"I'll bring Boat."

Michael climbed back on Mother's lap with Boat on one side and Dolly on the other.

Back and forth, back and forth, they rocked.

"I want my reindeer blanket," said Michael.

Carefully, Michael tucked his reindeer blanket around Boat and Dolly.

Back and forth, back and forth, they all rocked on Mother's lap.

"Puppy wants to come, too," said Michael.

Michael and Boat and Dolly and Puppy
all cuddled beneath the reindeer blanket
on Mother's lap.

Back and forth, back and forth, they
rocked.

"I hear Baby crying," said Mother.
"She'd like to rock, too."

"There isn't room," said Michael.

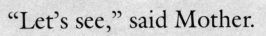

"Let's see," said Mother.

Michael and Baby both snuggled close to Mother. Boat and Dolly and Puppy were in Michael's arms, the reindeer blanket wrapped around them all. Back and forth, back and forth, they rocked.

"It feels good," said Michael.

His mother gave him a squeeze.
"You know, it's a funny thing," she whispered,
"but there is always room on Mother's lap."

Michael's favorite place to be is on Mother's lap,
cuddled close in her arms in the big rocking chair.
But is there room for his baby sister, too?

0-590-46889-8
SCHOLASTIC INC.
RL1 003-006